Dare to Care

PET
DRAGON

Original concept and illustrations by M.P. Robertson

Written by Sally Symes

Frances Lincoln
Children's Books

CONTENTS

Dare to Care for a Dragon?

As the Chief Dragon Officer
for the Royal Society for the
Prevention of Cruelty to Dragons,
it is my responsibility to inform you of
the pleasures and pitfalls of caring for one
of the world's most awesome creatures. This book
will teach you how to be a thoughtful and responsible
dragon owner. It will also help you to understand exactly
what you're letting yourself in for.
So, first things first. Before daring to care for a dragon,
you will need to consider the following:

Can you afford to feed it?

Is your house big enough?

Shopping list

- 1 cow
- 8 salmon
- 3 sheep
- 1 octopus
- 24 chickens
- 500 sausages

Dare to Care for a Dragon?

7

Dragonatomy

A responsible dragon-owner should take time to understand both the external and internal workings of these magnificent creatures.

BRAIN
Puce-green, wrinkled and not very big. Rarely used.

EARS
With acute hearing. Able to hear an ant burp from 20 miles away.

NOSE
Not used for smelling. Nostrils act as a vent for the fire pit in stomach. Long nostril hair and sticky mucus – used for catching tasty morsels which can be sniffed down later.

TENDRILS
Whiskery tendrils grow as male dragons mature. Can be styled to attract females.

TONGUE
Forked. Used for smelling and tasting. Rough surface to lick.

EYES
Pupils dilate according to light. They can see in the dark. The iris changes colour according to mood.

FEARSOME FACT
Dragon tears have healing properties. One drop is worth a fortune, but dragons rarely cry – they have nothing to be sad about.

VOCAL CHORDS
Dragons rarely speak, but they do sing. It is said that their song can hypnotise you. (Their roars however, can paralyse you.)

EYES COLOUR CODE

 YELLOW happy

 GREEN unwell

 BLUE sad

 RED angry

 BLACK get out of here!

JAWS
Very strong.

TASTE BUDS
Everything tastes sweet to a dragon.

HANDS
Four-fingered 'hands' with sharp, poisonous talons.

TEETH
Stabbers, biters and grinders for killing, tearing flesh and grinding bones. Bad odour, caused by poor hygiene and eating the wrong sort of food.

LUNGS

Huge, bellow-like structures. Perfect for making loud roars.

WINGS

Retractable, with sharp, claw-like finials. Dragons fly after they are a year old.

FEARSOME FACT

In days of yore, dragon heart-strings were used to make magical strings for bows.

BARBED BACKBONE

Sharp, spiny spikes for protection.

FEARSOME FACT

The pointy bit of a dragon's tail contains a venomous sting.

⚠ **KEEP YOUR DISTANCE**

TAIL

Used for balance and as a whip.

WARTS

Lots. Sometimes coloured. Often filled with pus.

STOMACH

Dragons have three stomachs.

1: FIRE PIT

This fire is constantly alight. Dragons breathe fire and burp gas simultaneously for maximum combustion.

2: GAS CHAMBER

Gas created by the breakdown of food is collected here. It can be expelled from either end.

3: MAIN STOMACH

Food eaten is broken down by acids over time. Some things take longer to digest than others (e.g. elephants).

DRAGON BLOOD

Cold, with supernatural powers.

FEET

Four toes – three front, one back toe.

Choosing a Breed

There are many different breeds of dragon, each with their own special characteristics. Before choosing one particular breed make sure that it is NOT any of the following...

TOO SMELLY

⚠ **TOXIC GAS**

THE PUDDLE LOAFER

With a diet of toxic pond weed and the occasional toad, this dragon emits foul odours from both ends of its corpulent body, making it impossible to live with.

TOO COLD

THE CHILLER

It is said that this dragon can freeze you with one look. It lives in countries with sub-zero temperatures – so don't go there if you're looking for a warm friendship.

TOO BIG

THE GARGANTUAN

Despite its colossal size, this dragon has a miniscule brain, making it too stupid to look where it's treading. Keep well away from this one.

DOWN!

TWO HEADED

THE IGNITER

This infernal duo may be very handy at lighting fires to keep your house warm, but they're not so hot at aiming, so you may not keep your house.

⚠ DOUBLE TROUBLE

Choosing an Egg

If you are daring enough to care for a dragon, we strongly advise that you start with an egg. Only buy dragon eggs from a reputable egg-thief. A good egg-thief should still have most of his limbs and at least a bit of common sense. A good egg-thief should listen to your requirements and help you choose the perfect dragon.

TOP TIP
Dragon eggs come in various sizes and colours according to their breed. Try to choose one that best suits your lifestyle. This isn't as easy as it looks... dragon thieves often muddle up eggs.

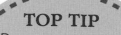

EGG STOLEN TOO NEAR HATCHING

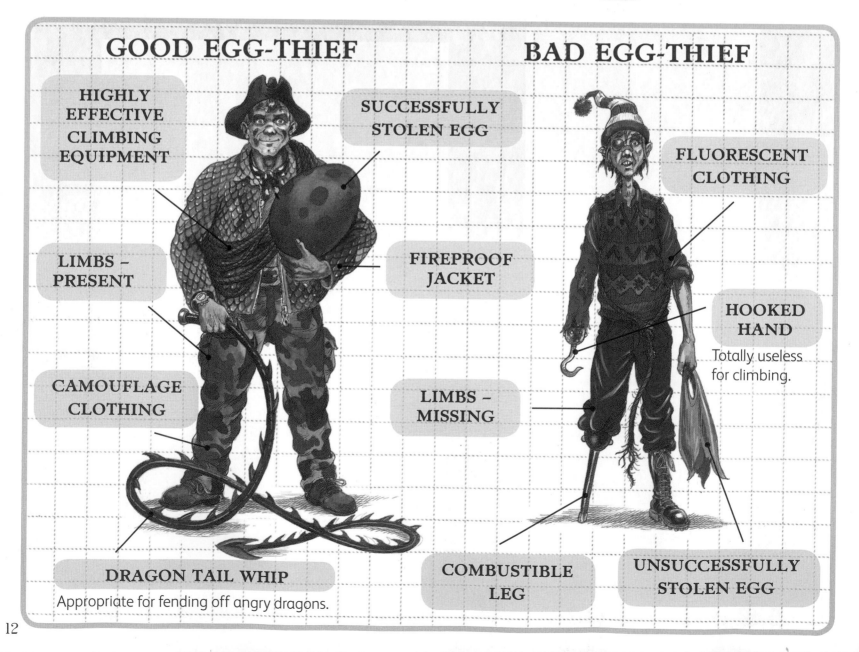

GOOD EGG-THIEF

HIGHLY EFFECTIVE CLIMBING EQUIPMENT

SUCCESSFULLY STOLEN EGG

LIMBS – PRESENT

FIREPROOF JACKET

CAMOUFLAGE CLOTHING

DRAGON TAIL WHIP
Appropriate for fending off angry dragons.

BAD EGG-THIEF

FLUORESCENT CLOTHING

HOOKED HAND
Totally useless for climbing.

LIMBS – MISSING

COMBUSTIBLE LEG

UNSUCCESSFULLY STOLEN EGG

NUTCASE STUDIES

Here are examples of some recent customers with their egg-purchases bought from *"Dragons Be Here,"* a specialist shop in Wales run by the notorious egg-thief, Ivor Scrooluce. Rodney, Harriet, Cassandra and Rick are all looking for their perfect dragon soul-mate. Let's see if Ivor can match them with the dragon of their dreams . . .

⚠ **CHOOSING THE RIGHT DRAGON EGG INVOLVES RISK. YOU NEVER KNOW WHAT YOU'RE GETTING UNTIL IT'S HATCHED.**

RODNEY

Likes a quiet life and a good book. He's partial to pies, prefers to read about adventures rather than participate and is good at solving puzzles.

Dream Dragon:
Swamp Lounger *(Swampus Slobellus)*
Characteristics – Docile, obedient and very greedy.

HARRIET

Likes a challenge and feeling the wind in her hair. She's down-to-earth but enjoys climbing, chocolate and getting into scrapes.

Dream Dragon:
Lightning Bolt *(Boltus Fugit)*
Characteristics – Fast, energetic and exhausting to be with.

CASSANDRA

Likes things to be neat, orderly and pink. She enjoys going to the gym, shopping and having the latest 'must-have' accessories.

Dream Dragon:
Dinky Diddums *(Precious Pinkus)*
Characteristics – Cute, pink and handbag-sized.

RICK

Doesn't mind a bit of pain or distress, especially when it's aimed at other people. He likes loud music, watching TV and chips.

Dream Dragon:
Ridgeback Savage *(Violentus Maximus)*
Characteristics – Big, fierce and slightly deranged.

Hatching Out

Once you have chosen your egg, take it home and put it in a warm, safe place, making sure that it is stored the right way up. We recommend that you talk to it regularly and play soothing music, just as our friends are doing here.

TOP TIP
Playing soothing music to a dragon egg results in a calmer baby dragon.

⚠️ LOUD BANGING NOISES CAN HAVE A DAMAGING EFFECT ON AN UNBORN DRAGON.

As a rule (but be aware, dragons don't usually obey rules), there are three stages to hatching:

GLOWING

RUMBLING

STEAMING

IN THE WILD

Dragons lay their eggs in the strangest places. Egg-thieves have found them behind waterfalls, deep inside sea caves, on the edge of volcanoes, up Mount Everest, in the Grand Canyon, and even on top of the Taj Mahal.

IN THE HOME

One owner had to vacate his bathroom for two years because his dragon had laid an egg on the toilet.

Hatching can take anywhere between two weeks and three years, so be prepared to be patient. It is imperative that you are present at the hatching, as dragons bond with the first thing they see…

MUMMY!

TOP TIP
Don't choose a long name – dragons have a short attention span.

Once your dragon has hatched, name it immediately and it will be your friend forever. (Unless you call it Fluffy.)

Cool Dragon Names

Ash	Flash	Pansy
Bernie	Flint	Pyromaniac
Blaise	Fry	Roast
Cracker	Frazzle	Rory
Crackle	Fury	Scorcha
Comet	Fernus	Sizzle
Drool	Fuse	Smokey
Ember	Fume	Sparky
Fang	Grind	Sparkle
Flame	Ignitious	Spike
Flaming	Infernando	Soar
Nora	Mortar	Toast
		Colin

Handling

Handling a baby dragon with its razor-sharp teeth and claws can be painful at times, so we firmly advise that you invest in the appropriate clothing. In days gone by, knights wore a suit of armour to protect against nips and scratches, but this could get quite hot at times.

CIRCA 1410

I'm roasting!

⚠ WHEN IT BITES — AND IT WILL — REMEMBER THAT YOUR DRAGON IS ONLY PLAYING. DO NOT RETALIATE! IT'S NEVER A GOOD IDEA TO LOSE YOUR HEAD.

BROOM

PROTECTIVE CLOTHING

A simple pair of falconry gloves and a welding helmet are the most effective way to pet your little creature without sustaining a serious wound. You might also find these other items helpful too:

WELDER'S MASK

SHIELD

Use a dustbin lid if you don't have a shield. (NB metal lids work better than plastic.)

FALCONER'S GLOVES

(heavy duty)

FIRE EXTINGUISHERS

FIRE BLANKET CAPE

DRAGON TREATS

FIREPROOF BROLLY

STURDY BOOTS

BODY LANGUAGE

Understanding your dragon's body language can increase your life expectancy, so it's good to recognise these basic emotions.

HAPPY

Head up, tail motionless, neck fringe down, eyes yellow, purring noise (like a pneumatic drill).

CROSS

Head down, tail flicking, neck fringe raised, eyes red, grrrring noise (like 50 pneumatic drills), teeth bared.

PURRRRR

Nice healthy din-dins for Fluffy!

INCANDESCENT WITH RAGE

Mouth wide, tail whipping, neck fringe huge, eyes black, wings unfurled, emits fire from mouth.

GRRRRRR

TOP TIP
Never feed salad to a Ridgeback Savage.

Feeding

It is imperative that your dragon has a regular feeding routine. Food is required every 15 minutes for the first year, then every 30 minutes thereafter. Failure to provide enough nourishment for your pet could result in death – most probably yours (humans make extremely tasty dragon-snacks).

A Balanced Diet

MINERALS

Dragons literally do require actual 'fuel' for their bodies. As fire-breathing creatures, they need a regular supply of sulphur, coal and flint to keep the flame in their stomach alight.

SULPHUR

COAL

FLINT

VEGETABLES

Dragons need a varied diet, so make sure they eat enough vegetables. They particularly like chilli peppers, horseradish and mustard plants... with a sprinkling of black pepper.

ANIMALS

Dragons eat anything, but they especially like meat, so access to a regular local source of meat is essential. (No need for cooking or chopping. Dragons eat their meat just as it comes.)

⚠ NEVER FEED BRUSSELS SPROUTS TO A DRAGON.

BABY FOOD

A newly-hatched dragon should be fed small amounts of solid food straight away. Start them off with a few roughly mashed rats, then gradually increase the amount and variety of food in their first year until they build up to eating three or four large cows (no need to mash these).

DRINK

Dragons only drink water, preferably dirty.

Foods to Avoid

SWEETS

It is not a good idea to give your pet dragon sweeties as
a) Sugar makes them hyperactive and difficult to handle.
b) It rots their teeth – and a dragon with toothache is impossible to handle.

CURRY

They may like it at the time, but you'll pay for it later.

Grooming

Keeping your dragon looking good can be a time-consuming and expensive business. There are specialist dragon-grooming parlours scattered about the world, but these are mostly reserved for the A-list celebrity dragon-owners and are extremely costly. Just look how many people are involved in dragon-grooming...

PLUMBER

If your dragon has a blockage, he's your man.

TILER

Great for fixing dislodged scales.

PEST CONTROL

Brilliant for keeping dragon fleas in check.

PAINTER-DECORATOR

For fancying-up those manicured talons.

CHIMNEY SWEEP

Excellent for clearing nostrils of cinders and bogeys.

CLEANING CREW

Just the job for adding sparkle and shine to scales and wings.

WINDOW CLEANER

Perfect for cleaning teeth.

PRESSURE WASHING

The best way to remove tongue grime and keep your dragon's breath fresh.

TREE SURGEON

Terrific for keeping claws in check.

⚠ **MAKE SURE EVERYONE IS INSURED.**

Taking Your Dragon to the Vet

Dragons don't often succumb to illness, but if your pet is unwell, you may need to take it to a vet.

TOP TIP
Ask for the dragon-specialist when you ring for an appointment. A budgie-specialist will not do.

A VET IS TRAINED TO...

diagnose the problem, then...

Say AHH.

HELP!

I think he was hungry!

...make it better.

Common Dragon Ailments

WORMS

Symptoms: flatulence, wriggling stuff in poo.

FLEAS

Symptoms: constant scratching, sore patches on skin.

INGROWING CLAWS

Symptoms: difficulty walking, throbbing feet – sometimes caused by claw-biting.

TICKS

Symptoms: none. Ticks will gorge themselves, then explode, so catch them before they make a big mess on your carpet.

THERE you are, Fifi!

VOMITING

Symptoms: being sick. This usually happens when dragons have eaten something that disagrees with them.

FLU

Symptoms: hacking cough, sneezing, high temperature and an excess of mucus.

Bless you!

⚠ DRAGON MUCUS IS AS HOT AS LAVA

Exercise and Training

Dragons need regular exercise, but taking one out is no walk in the park, especially if you plan to go somewhere public like a... er... park.

Training

Compared to the size of their bodies, dragons' brains are miniscule and hold very little intelligence. As a consequence, they are NOT the easiest pet to train. However, with a lot of patience, kindness and food, you can teach them to respond to simple commands such as:

SIT

HEEL

TOP TIP
Use a stern, firm tone of voice to reprimand your dragon if it misbehaves. Never shout, or you will lose your voice (and the rest of your body).

That wasn't quite what I meant.

Not again.

FETCH

Go, boy!

24

Be Prepared

You will need to take your specialised equipment with you on your walks: a large collar and lead (attached firmly to your dragon), a fireproof poop scoop, 9 or 10 fireproof poop bags, a few treats, 2 one-ton foot-weights and a couple of good friends.

NOSTRIL CORKS

FIREPROOF MUZZLE

STRONG COLLAR AND LEAD

(firmly buckled).

FIREPROOF POOP BAGS

and one fireproof poop scoop (large).

FIRE EXTINGUISHER

in case of little accidents.

ANKLE WEIGHTS

to keep your dragon down to earth.

DROP

Oh dear.

TOP TIP
Give your pet the respect it deserves and you will have it eating out of your hand in no time. (Do this carefully, or it may actually eat your hand.)

Flight School

Once you have some sort of control over your dragon on the ground, you may want to try flying it. But before taking to the skies, you must have lessons with a licensed instructor and pass your dragon-flying test.

TOP TIP
Once you have passed your test, allow the dragon to set fire to your L plates. But remove them from your body first.

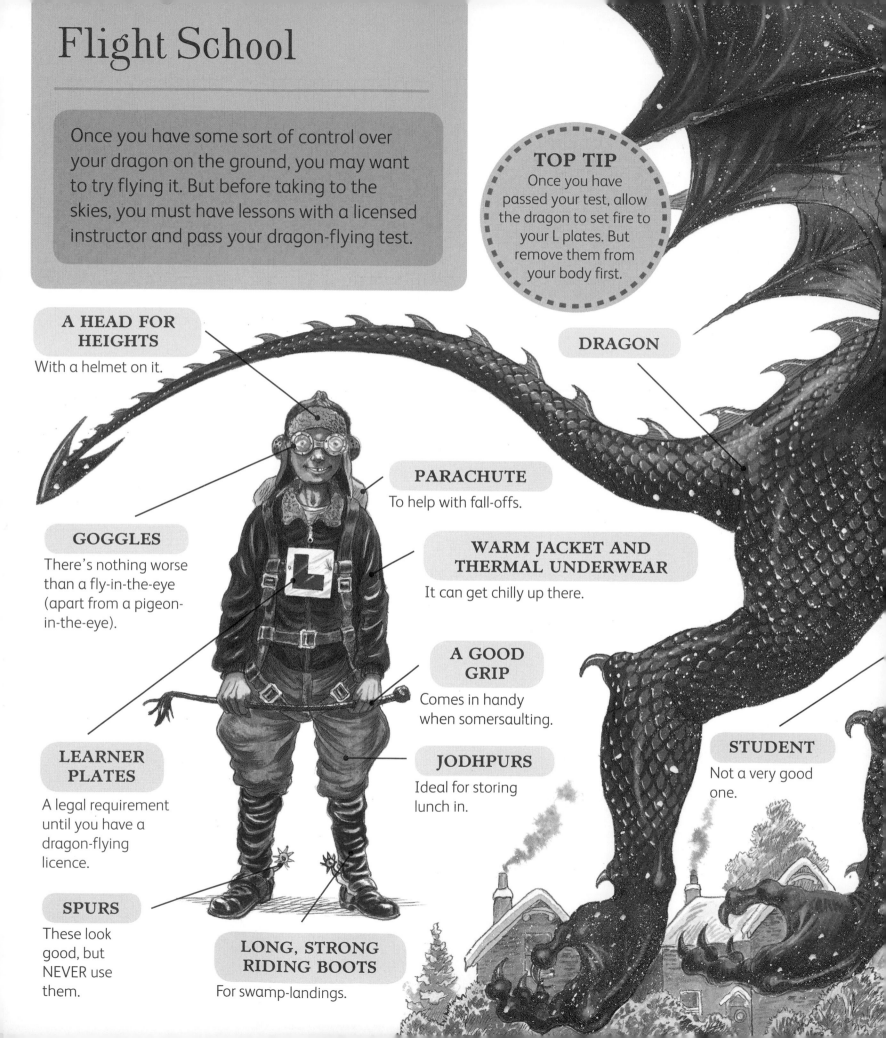

A HEAD FOR HEIGHTS

With a helmet on it.

DRAGON

PARACHUTE

To help with fall-offs.

GOGGLES

There's nothing worse than a fly-in-the-eye (apart from a pigeon-in-the-eye).

WARM JACKET AND THERMAL UNDERWEAR

It can get chilly up there.

A GOOD GRIP

Comes in handy when somersaulting.

LEARNER PLATES

A legal requirement until you have a dragon-flying licence.

JODHPURS

Ideal for storing lunch in.

STUDENT

Not a very good one.

SPURS

These look good, but NEVER use them.

LONG, STRONG RIDING BOOTS

For swamp-landings.

BIT

BRIDLE

SADDLE

REINS

FLYING
INSTRUCTOR

☑ Take-off
☑ Fly straight
☑ Overtake
☑ Emergency stop
☑ Loop-the-loop
☑ Landing safely

A LONG
LADDER

For mounting
your steed.

PASSING YOUR TEST

When you have trained daily
for at least a year, you will be
ready to take your test. In order
to pass, you must master the
following: **take-off** (without
falling off), **flying** (in a straight
line), **overtaking** (mainly
pigeons and planes), **keeping
to the speed limit** (333 mph),
emergency stops (difficult
at 333 mph), **loop-the-loops**
(without vomiting), and **landing
safely** (NOT on a house).

27

The Sky's the Limit

Remember, the first few years with your dragon will be tricky, but if you survive them, you will travel the world, see places you could never imagine, make friends with people in very high places, and never, ever have to struggle to light a barbecue again. Treat your dragon well, and you will have a friend for life... and longer. Good luck!

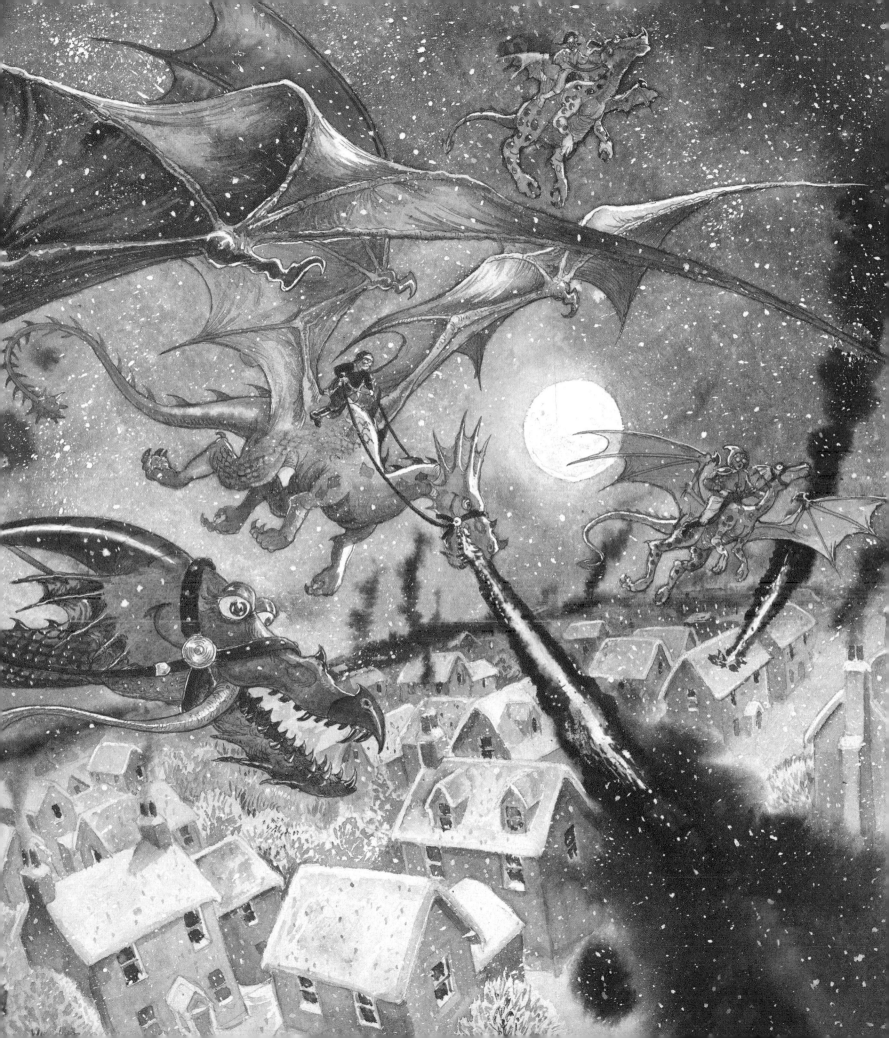

To find out more about M.P. Robertson or to book him for an event
please visit www.mprobertson.com

Quarto is the authority on a wide range of topics.
Quarto educates, entertains and enriches the lives of
our readers—enthusiasts and lovers of hands-on living.
www.quartoknows.com

JANETTA OTTER-BARRY BOOKS

First published in Great Britain and in the USA in 2016 by
Frances Lincoln Children's Books, 74-77 White Lion Street, London N1 9PF
QuartoKnows.com
Visit our blogs at QuartoKnows.com

A catalogue record for this book is available from the British Library.

ISBN 978-1-84780-589-8

Printed in China

3 5 7 9 8 6 4